DECEMBER

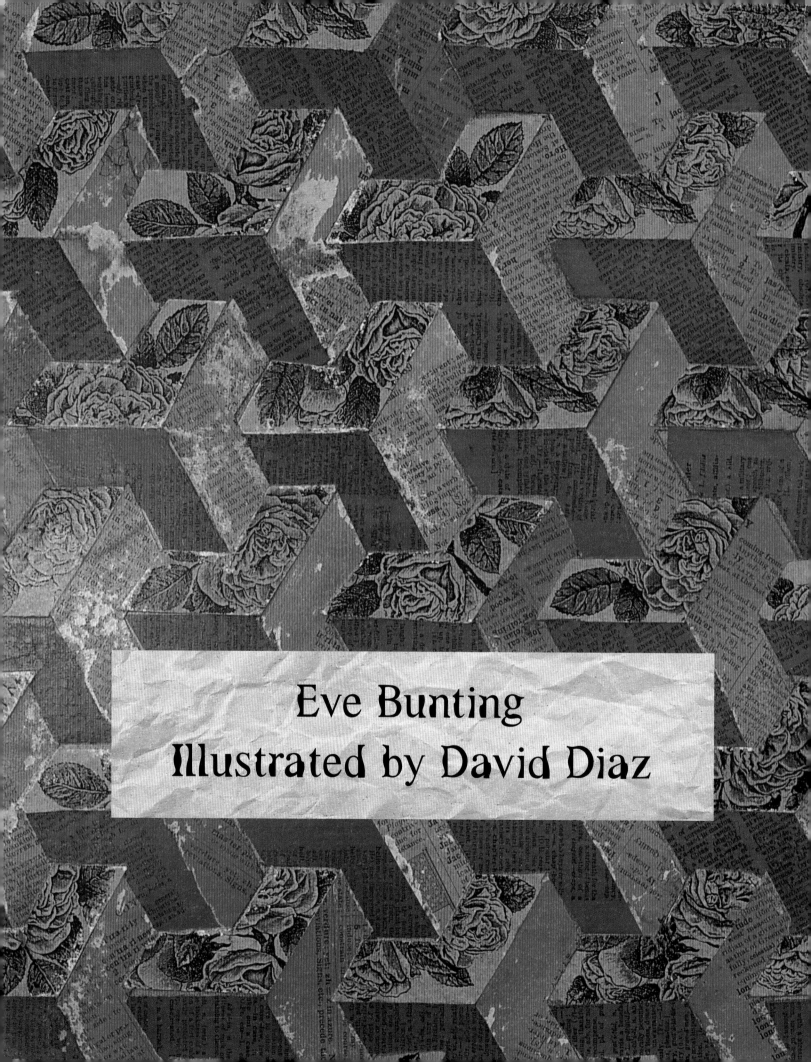

Eve Bunting
Illustrated by David Diaz

DECEMBER

VOYAGER BOOKS
HARCOURT, INC.
SAN DIEGO   NEW YORK   LONDON

www.harcourtbooks.com

First Voyager Books edition 2000
Voyager Books is a registered trademark of Harcourt, Inc.

Library of Congress has catalogued the hardcover edition as follows:
Bunting, Eve, 1928–
December/Eve Bunting; illustrated by David Diaz.
p. cm.
Summary: A homeless family's luck changes after they help an
old woman who has even less than they do at Christmas.
[1. Christmas—Fiction. 2. Homeless persons—Fiction.]
I. Diaz, David, ill. II. Title.
PZ7.B91527Df 1997
[Fic]—dc20   96-21148
ISBN 0-15-201434-9

ISBN 0-15-202422-0 pb

E G I K L J H F

To my grandchildren—
"For you have the faces of angels."
—E. B.

For Ana
—D. D.

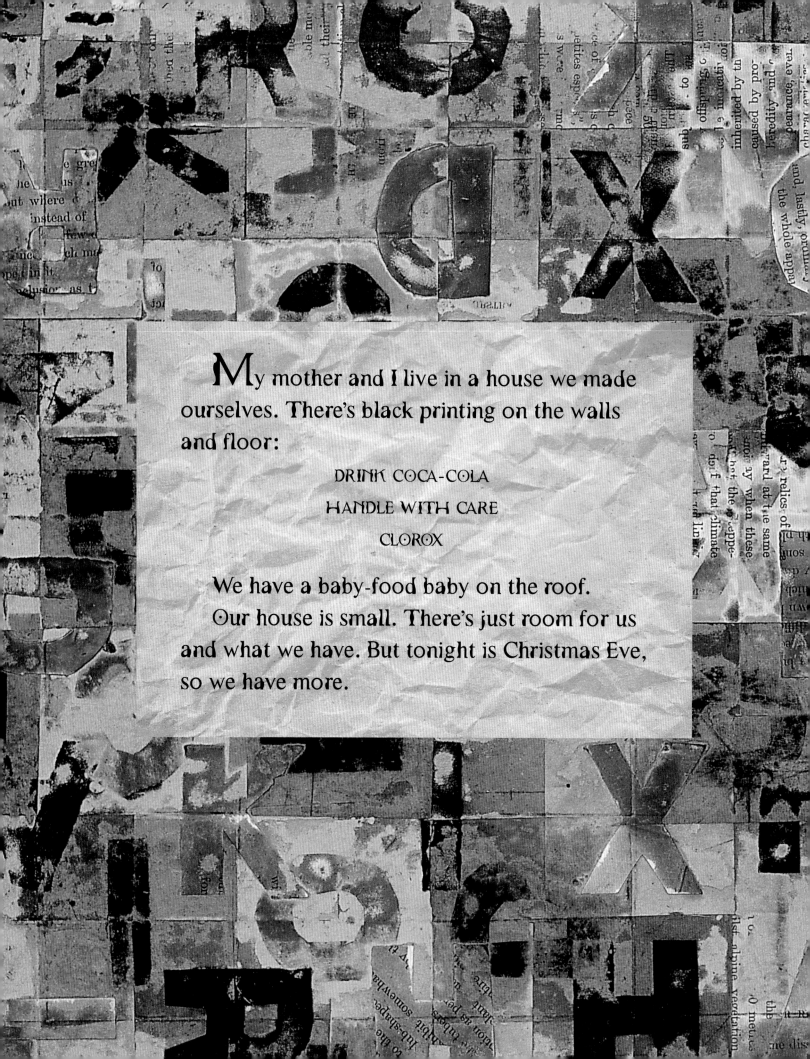

My mother and I live in a house we made ourselves. There's black printing on the walls and floor:

DRINK COCA-COLA

HANDLE WITH CARE

CLOROX

We have a baby-food baby on the roof.
Our house is small. There's just room for us and what we have. But tonight is Christmas Eve, so we have more.

We have a tiny tree. It's the top of a real tree the Christmas lot man gave us. We've hung it with neat things. A toy soldier I've kept since I was little. A shiny, silvery spoon. Beads from a necklace I once found on the sidewalk. And Mom has made a star for the top.

Under the tree on a paper Santa plate are our two Christmas cookies, one red, one green. The green one is mine. I collected thirty-two soda pop cans and took them to John's Market to get those cookies. John gave me the plate.

On our wooden crate are Mary, the baby, one shepherd, one sheep. We tried to make the soldier be Joseph, but he didn't look right. We have a fat red candle, too.

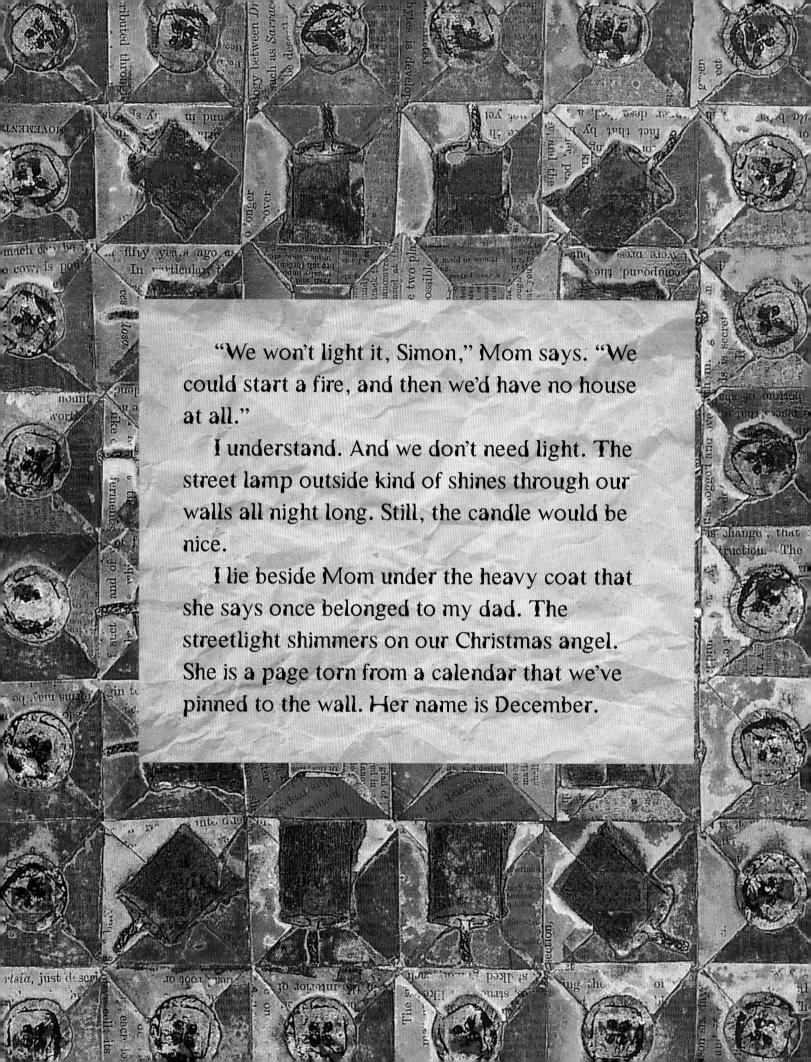

"We won't light it, Simon," Mom says. "We could start a fire, and then we'd have no house at all."

I understand. And we don't need light. The street lamp outside kind of shines through our walls all night long. Still, the candle would be nice.

I lie beside Mom under the heavy coat that she says once belonged to my dad. The streetlight shimmers on our Christmas angel. She is a page torn from a calendar that we've pinned to the wall. Her name is December.

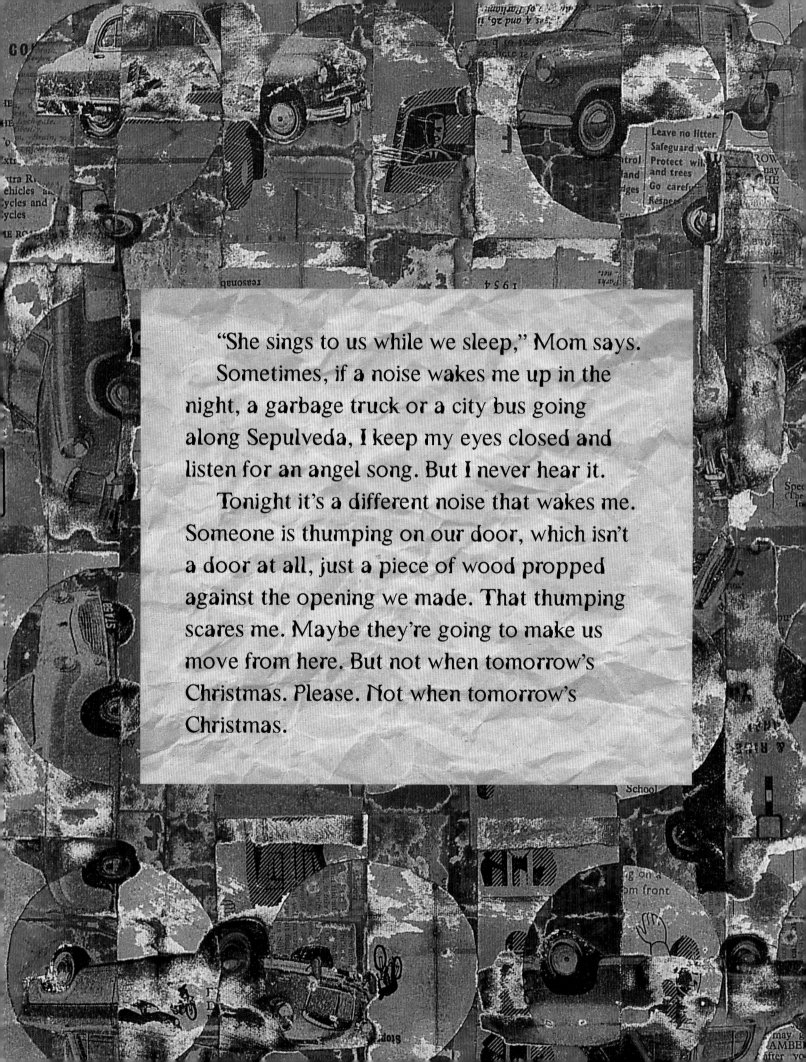

"She sings to us while we sleep," Mom says.

Sometimes, if a noise wakes me up in the night, a garbage truck or a city bus going along Sepulveda, I keep my eyes closed and listen for an angel song. But I never hear it.

Tonight it's a different noise that wakes me. Someone is thumping on our door, which isn't a door at all, just a piece of wood propped against the opening we made. That thumping scares me. Maybe they're going to make us move from here. But not when tomorrow's Christmas. Please. Not when tomorrow's Christmas.

Thump! Thump!

My heart thumps, too.

"Who's there?" Mom stands and tries to push me behind her, but I get in front. I always look after her.

"Who's there?"

Nobody answers.

Mom slides the wood so she can peer out, then lifts the door away.

I see an old woman. She's half-hidden in clothes on top of clothes. Her black hat has a fake rose pinned to it.

"Can I come in?" she asks. "I'm so cold."

Mom looks her over carefully. On the streets we have to be careful. Then she takes the old woman's arm. "Come on in."

The woman is bent way over. But I think that's how she is, and not because our roof is so low. Sometimes I'm afraid my mom will get to be bent like that.

"Can I sleep here tonight?" the woman asks.

"Yes." Mom takes the coat that is still warm from being over us. "Wrap up in this."

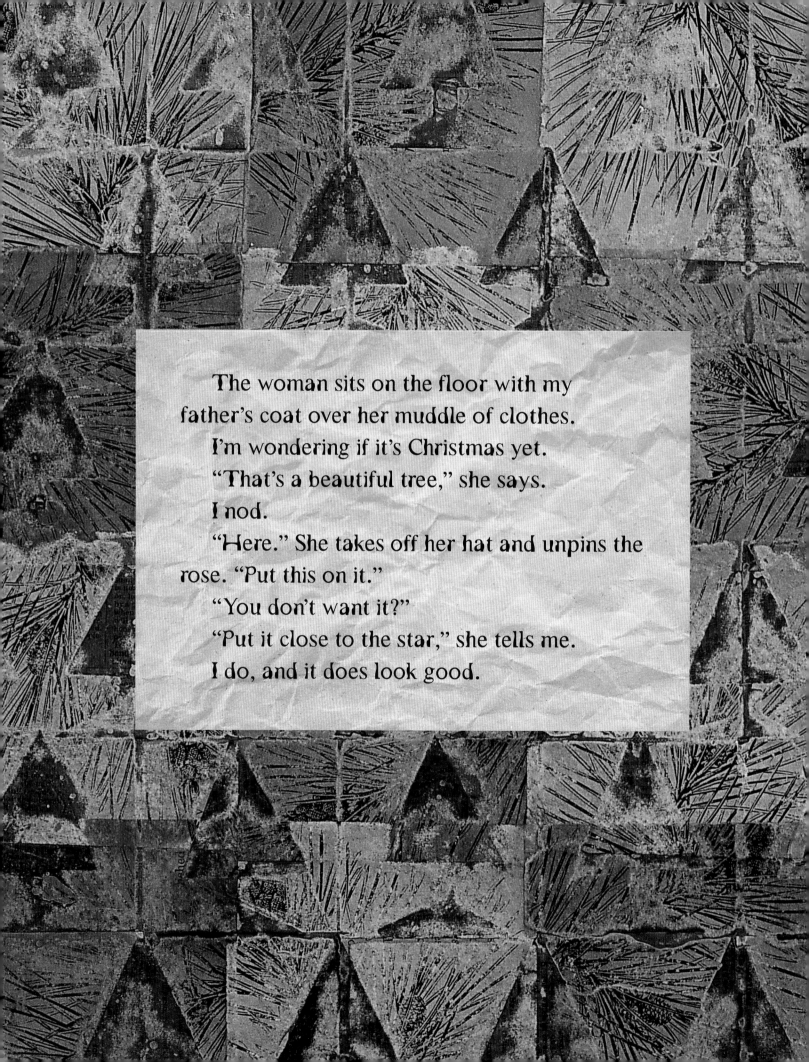

The woman sits on the floor with my
father's coat over her muddle of clothes.
   I'm wondering if it's Christmas yet.
   "That's a beautiful tree," she says.
   I nod.
   "Here." She takes off her hat and unpins the
rose. "Put this on it."
   "You don't want it?"
   "Put it close to the star," she tells me.
   I do, and it does look good.

I see her staring at the cookies. She's probably hungry. She swallows, and her neck is so thin I can watch the swallow going down. I think of something very nice that I could do but I try not to listen to the thought, and I don't want to do it. I put out my hand, pull it back, put it out again, and lift the Santa plate. "Have the green one," I say.

She takes it slowly, eats it slowly.

I try hard not to think of all those soda cans.

Mom smiles at me. I'm glad when she doesn't offer to give up her red cookie, too, because I'm pretty sure tomorrow we'll go halfers.

There's just enough room for the three of us to lie side by side.

"It's warm in here," the old woman says. She smiles. "It's warm with love."

Maybe. But still, I miss the weight of my dad's coat over us. I miss the HIM smell, even though I don't remember him. I curl as close to Mom as I can.

The traffic outside is not as loud as usual. Christmas Eve.

And I sleep.

When I wake up it's morning and the street lamp is off. Shadows lie in our cardboard house. I start to wake Mom to say "Merry Christmas!" when I remember the old woman.

She's gone. My father's coat is neatly folded. Maybe I'm not *that* nice because I look quickly to check if the red cookie is still there. It is.

The woman hasn't put the wood back to close our door, so I get up and I see a dim figure in the opening. Was she there all the time? It's not the woman, though. It's our angel, December. It can't be! I know I'm dreaming. I rub my eyes and look again. She's still there. But I can see the calendar page. She's still on our wall, too. How can that be?

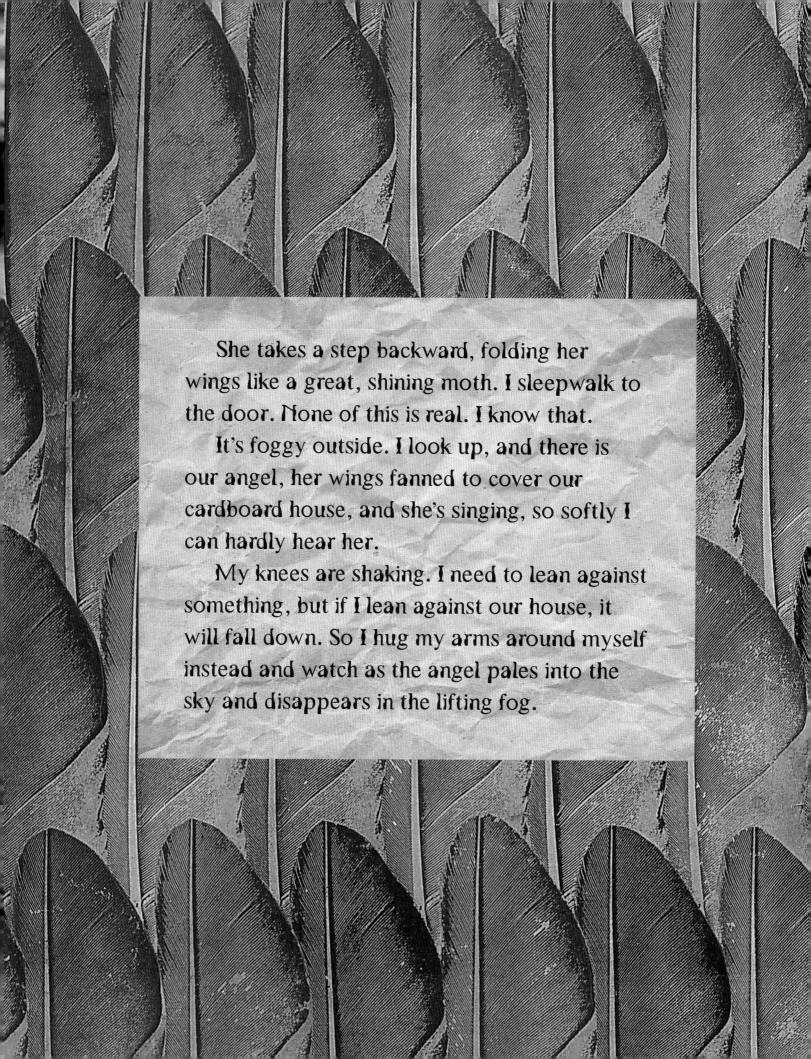

She takes a step backward, folding her wings like a great, shining moth. I sleepwalk to the door. None of this is real. I know that.

It's foggy outside. I look up, and there is our angel, her wings fanned to cover our cardboard house, and she's singing, so softly I can hardly hear her.

My knees are shaking. I need to lean against something, but if I lean against our house, it will fall down. So I hug my arms around myself instead and watch as the angel pales into the sky and disappears in the lifting fog.

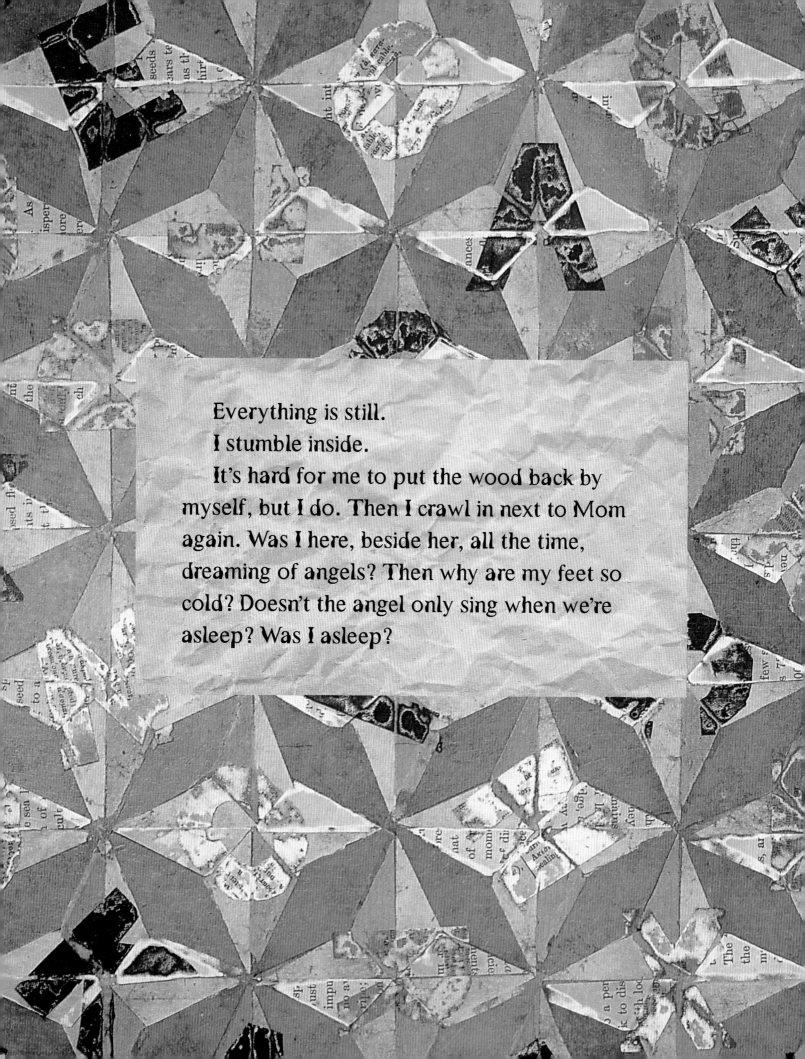

Everything is still.

I stumble inside.

It's hard for me to put the wood back by myself, but I do. Then I crawl in next to Mom again. Was I here, beside her, all the time, dreaming of angels? Then why are my feet so cold? Doesn't the angel only sing when we're asleep? Was I asleep?

It's strange how everything started to change for us after that. People would say our luck just turned. Maybe. But I don't think so.

Now it's another Christmas Eve, and Mom has been working since summer. We have an apartment in the projects, two floors up, with real walls. We have a tiny tree. On its branches hang a toy soldier, a silvery spoon, the beads I once found on the sidewalk, and the crumpled fake rose. Under the tree is a paper plate with two cookies, one red and one green. On our crate are the red candle, Mary, the baby, one shepherd, one sheep...and Joseph.

December smiles down at us from her place on the wall. I never noticed until after last Christmas Eve, but if you look real closely you can see she has a faded rose in her hair.

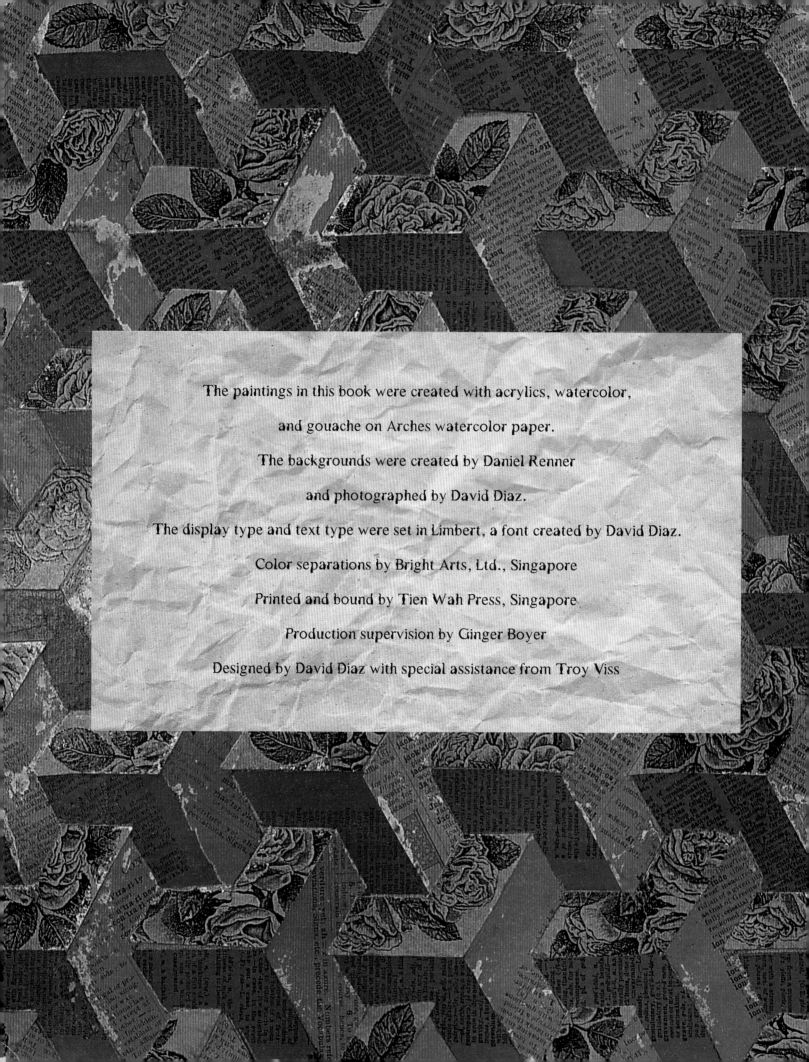

The paintings in this book were created with acrylics, watercolor,

and gouache on Arches watercolor paper.

The backgrounds were created by Daniel Renner

and photographed by David Diaz.

The display type and text type were set in Limbert, a font created by David Diaz.

Color separations by Bright Arts, Ltd., Singapore

Printed and bound by Tien Wah Press, Singapore

Production supervision by Ginger Boyer

Designed by David Diaz with special assistance from Troy Viss